Copyright © 2012/2021 by Jannette Quackenbush
ISBN-13 : 978-1940087078

All rights reserved. No part of this book may be reproduced or transmitted in any form or by any means, electronic or mechanical, including photocopying, recording, or by any information storage and retrieval system, without permission in writing from the copyright owner.

This is a work of fiction. Names, characters, places and incidents either are the product of the author's imagination or are used fictitiously, and any resemblance to any actual persons, living or dead, events, or locales is entirely coincidental. This book was printed in the United States of America.
Columbus Skyline Image: David Mark

I0630232

Table of Contents

Haunted Old Cemeteries

Haunted Buildings

Haunted River Areas

Haunted Parks

Haunted Bars & Restaurants

Haunted Railways and Roadways

Haunted Colleges

Not Far from Columbus . . .

Haunted Old Cemeteries

Old Franklinton Cemetery
(Old Sullivant Cemetery)
N Davis Avenue
Columbus, Ohio 43222
39.962852, -83.022225

The Return

There is an ancient burial ground along a bend in the Scioto River just off McKinley Avenue. Occasionally, a strange fog seeps up from the surrounding streets and creeps its way into the cemetery. From the mist, a ghostly man emerges for only a few moments, pacing back and forth before he disappears. Many believe this ghost is the town's founder.

In 1797, Lucas Sullivant established a small village here along the Scioto River, called it Franklinton, and it eventually grew into Columbus. When the town was only a couple of years old, the first burial took place in its cemetery. Over the years, townspeople added a church, and many more were laid to rest in the graveyard, including Sullivant. His corpse was later removed and taken to Green Lawn Cemetery. Now he returns to where his body once laid as if searching for something left behind.

North Market
(Old North Cemetery)
59 Spruce Street
Columbus, Ohio 43215
39.972228,-83.004355

The Forsaken

The Old North Graveyard was one of the earliest cemeteries established in 1813 by a 2-acre donation from a man named Kerr. It grew to 10 acres and was filled with early settlers and their offspring and families who remained inhabitants of the growing city. As time passed, the city decided this land would be better suited for development. So some of the corpses were dug up and moved to other cemeteries. Most were not. Years later, the land became part of a parking lot and The North Market.

People passing by have always been troubled by an old resident of the boneyard lingering where the forsaken cemetery still sits below a parking lot and buildings. He is a sharply dressed man walking the area on foggy early mornings with a lantern in his hand, searching intently for something before he disappears. Most believe it to be Kerr who, along with his wife and young children, died during an epidemic and was buried here, but his body was never found when digging up the graves to move to another cemetery.

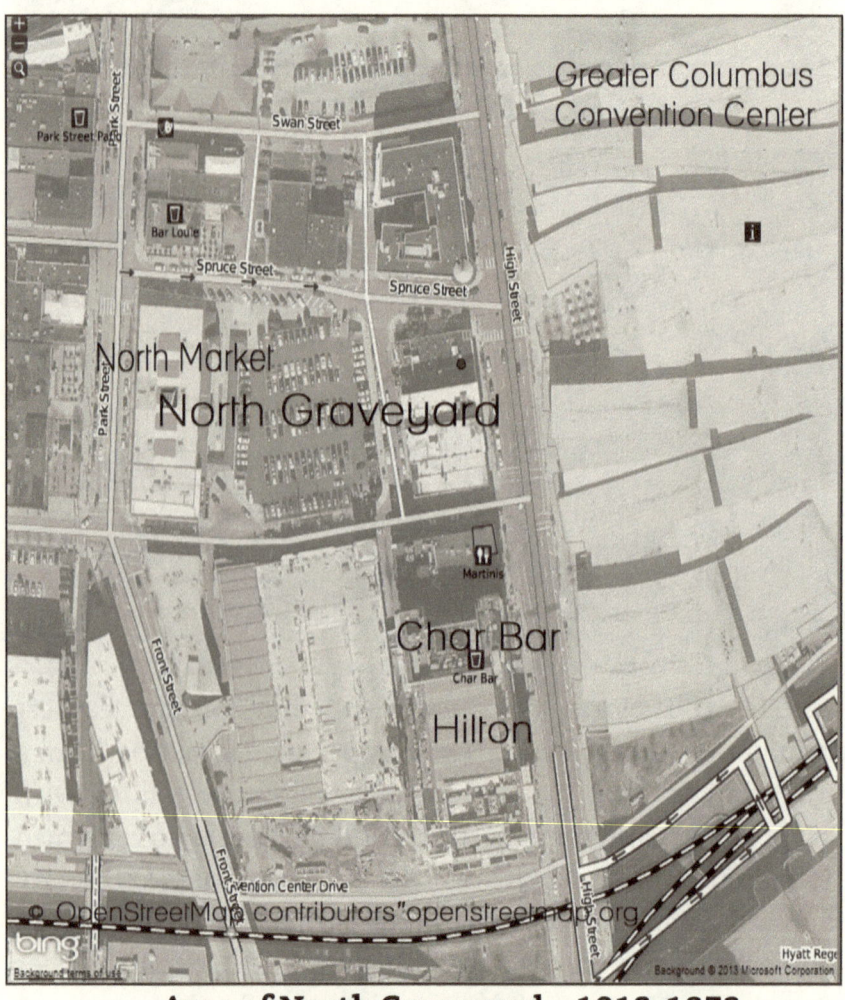

Area of North Graveyard—1813-1873
(Some bodies moved to Green Lawn)

Camp Chase Cemetery
Sullivant Avenue
Columbus, Ohio 43204
39.943881,-83.075953

Veiled Lady

Camp Chase during the Civil War.

In Columbus, the Hilltop subdivision was once a training encampment for Union recruits called Camp Chase and later a prisoner of war camp holding enlisted Confederates. When the camp closed after the war, Quakers purchased the property as a settlement. Within a couple of years of the end of the war, the structures for the camp were dismantled.

The Confederate prisoners' cemetery, then on a lonely dirt road called Sullivant's Free Pike and near the area of the camp pest house, was abandoned and left overridden with weeds.

Camp Chase Cemetery—late 1800s.

Travelers passing by noted a lady in a gray dress and veil walking through the cemetery during those years. She was heard crying softly to herself and, at times, tossed flowers and petals on the graves. Most went on, leaving her politely to her grief. However, others whispered shaming words about her; the wounds from the war were still fresh, and some held disdain for the dead rebels there. But few knew the mysterious woman's identity until many years later.

Louisiana Ransburg Briggs, a young woman from Missouri, was sent to be schooled at Ohio Wesleyan to save her from the ravages of war in the south. Some classmates disliked her for being openly supportive of the south. She met her future husband, Joseph Briggs—prominent Franklin County landowner, while at the school, marrying him in 1867 at age 17.

A few years after her marriage, she discovered the cemetery. For ten years, she courageously scattered flowers amongst the neglected graves wearing a veil to hide her identity and save her husband's reputation from being marred. Over the years and with the aid of William Knauss, a former Union soldier, the cemetery was cleaned, and memorial services began.

Camp Chase Cemetery today.

Camp Chase was, like most prison camps, overcrowded. Some of the confined soldiers there died from smallpox (many in an 1863 - 1864 epidemic), cholera, and starvation. Over 2,168 Confederate soldiers were buried in the Camp Chase Cemetery.

She still walks among the graves. Passersby have seen a ghostly woman strolling within the cemetery in dark clothing and veil. When they pause in their steps to ponder her strange garb, she disappears.

Nationwide Children's Hospital/Livingston Park
(aka: Columbus City Cemetery, East Graveyard, Old East Graveyard, South Graveyard)
S 18th Street
Columbus, Ohio 43205
39.953043, -82.976486

The Unclaimed

The area of an old cemetery, now gone.

An aged cemetery lies hidden beneath a park in Columbus. It began as 11 1/4 swampy acres on Livingston Avenue and Eighteenth Street in 1839, and within ten years, the city added a dead house to store corpses until burial. The city sold lots in the front to residents, while the rear became a burial ground for the public, which from 1862 to 1863, prison authorities had 22 Confederate prisoners from Camp Chase interred here.

People like James Broome were buried in the lot too. He left his family in Pennsylvania, got drunk on bad whiskey, and died during his stay one night in jail. His body was taken to the dead house, but nobody ever claimed him. Nobody claimed Birdie May either. She was buried at the cemetery too in 1871, a young woman who boarded at what a newspaper referred to as "Sue Stump's disrespectable house on Strawberry Alley." Birdie returned one late evening, cried out, "I'm dying, I'm dying!" and fell back to the floor dead. James Taylor was in his early twenties and worked on a canal boat before he ended up in the old yard for the dead. One afternoon he decided to cool off in the Scioto River, but a cramp seized him; he disappeared under the water and never came back up on his own. His family hailed from England, and, being mid-August, the body needed to be entombed quickly, so he was buried in the old cemetery with all the others unclaimed.

By 1873, the cemetery name had been changed from South Cemetery to East Cemetery. It had fallen into disrepair with broken fences and headstones, uncut grass, and only the poor and paupers were laid to rest beneath the ground. It was closed in the mid-1870s and declared a park, South Park, and later renamed Livingston Park. Some of the 2,344 known graves were removed. Still, the actual number of the dead beneath the soil would never be known as many were buried there without approval. Some stones were still remaining into the late 1950s when workers dumped them to support the banks of Alum Creek during a flood. Many years have passed since the graveyard was filled with the newly departed. Occasionally those enjoying themselves at Livingston Park or visiting Children's Hospital see a woman in a pink dress strolling through the grass, crying, and appearing to look hard for something on the ground. She is so intent, some have nearly gotten close enough to touch her before she vanishes.

Area of Old East Graveyard 1839-1860
(Some bodies moved to Green Lawn)

Green Lawn Abbey
Woodlawn Mausoleum
700 Greenlawn Avenue
Columbus, Ohio 43223
39.940780, -83.016102

The Magician's Final Trick

Green Lawn Abbey is a private mausoleum originally built in 1927. It has 572 crypts and one that holds not only a corpse but also a ghost. Howard Thurston, who billed himself as the 'King of Cards' for his talent with magic card tricks, haunts the abbey. Thurston, the son of a carriage maker in Columbus, grew up performing card tricks and eventually took his talent on the road during the early 1900s vaudeville era. While performing in Charleston, West Virginia, he suffered a cerebral hemorrhage and, less than a year later, died from a stroke at age 66. His family buried him in the mausoleum in 1936. Since then, visitors to the cemetery have seen his ghost strolling around the property.

Green Lawn Cemetery
Hayden Mausoleum
1000 Greenlawn Avenue
Columbus, Ohio 43223
39.939143, -83.033255

Knock-Knock

Built for Charles H. Hayden, Columbus banker, the Hayden Mausoleum is haunted. If you knock on the door, you can hear a knocking in return!

Section 87, Grave Plot 243
James Howard
1000 Greenlawn Avenue
Columbus, Ohio 43223
39.939143, -83.033255

The Ghastly Crime of Doctor Snook

Snook.

There is a grave that most can only find by seeing the ghost who hovers over it. It is concealed and for a good reason because something wicked lies beneath and hovers nearby. The man who is buried here was convicted of a horrible crime.

In June of 1929, James Howard Snook was a respected Ohio State University professor in the College of Veterinary Medicine. He appeared to be a devoted husband and father of a young daughter. But Snook held a shocking secret—for three years, he had been having a sordid affair with a 24-year-old college student, Theora Hix, whom he had met while she worked as a stenographer at the school, to cover her room and board costs. The two often enjoyed pretending to be a married couple. Snook played the role of a salt salesman meeting his young wife at Missus Margaret Smalley's small rooming house on Hubbard Avenue in downtown Columbus. They would also slip off into the countryside, taking long rides before finding a secluded area. Nobody would have, most likely, ever discovered the clandestine affair if Snook had not, in a fit of rage, murdered Hix at one of those isolated areas one evening—the New York Central Rifle Range on Fisher Road near McKinley Avenue. Her badly beaten body was found by two 16-year-old North High School boys the next day. Not long after several persons identified her body and personal items, Snook was brought in for questioning and arrested. He was later convicted and received the death penalty.

The professor had dinner with his wife right before he walked into the death chamber. "My peace is absolutely made with my God," he muttered before he died in the electric chair at the Ohio State Penitentiary. It is not true. For many years, to stop what the newspapers described as the "morbidly curious" from viewing or desecrating the grave, the location of his headstone was kept confidential by the cemetery after a short, early morning funeral at Green Lawn. His small gravestone did not state his last name, simply James Howard. But occasionally, you can find the marker. Visitors to the cemetery have witnessed Snook's ghost hovering around it. He appears riled and relenting and in the same agitated state that left him murdering his mistress.

Leatherlips' Grave
10994-11000 Riverside Drive
Powell, Ohio 43065
40.140056,-83.118454

Leatherlips

The place where a ghost rises.

Shateyaronya, a Wyandot who lived in Ohio, haunts the area around the Scioto River. His ghost is explained like this—

In 1808, John Sells settled with his wife in a log cabin on 400 acres along the west bank of the Scioto River. Within a year, he started the Black Horse Tavern, named for a horse he purchased in Kentucky a few years earlier. The tavern was a popular stopover for those traveling along the Scioto.

A frequent visitor was a Wyandot Chief by the name of Shateyaronya, nicknamed Chief Leatherlips because it was said his spoken words were as strong as leather. When Chief Leatherlips was building his friendship with the Sells, central Ohio was filled with friendly and hostile Indians. A war had been stewing with a large confederation led by Tecumseh against the United States over farmers settling on land used by his people. But Leatherlips refused to unite with Tecumseh and refused to turn his back on his white friends along the Scioto. When many of the Wyandotte moved to northern Ohio, a safer distance from the settlers, disease and bad luck seemed to follow. They blamed Leatherlips for their ill-fortune and said he had cursed them. A delegation came to hunt Leatherlips down and bring him and his remaining followers back to the Wyandotte tribe or, if they refused, to massacre them.

John Sells tried to barter with the Wyandotte, using a horse to trade for the leader's life. But the Wyandotte swore he used witchcraft to curse them, and he was to be executed. After some discourse, John Sells' pleas were rejected by those who intended to kill Chief Leatherlips. Otway Curry, a Hesperian monthly magazine journalist, described Leatherlips' death as: *He washed himself and donned fresh clothing. Then Leatherlips knelt down at a shallow grave previously prepared by the Wyandotte and prayed. Suddenly one of the warriors drew from beneath the skirts of his capote, a keen, bright tomahawk, walked rapidly up behind the chieftain brandishing the weapon on high for a single moment and then struck with his full strength. The blow descended directly upon the crown of the head, and the victim immediately fell prostrate. After he had lain a while in the agonies of death, the Indian directed the attention of the white men to the drops of sweat which were gathering upon the neck and face, remarking with much apparent exultation that it was conclusive proof of the sufferer's guilt.*

Again the executioner advanced and with the same weapon inflicted two or three additional and heavy blows. As soon as life was entirely extinct, the body was hastily buried with all its apparel and decorations and the assemblage dispersed. The Wyandot returned immediately to their hunting grounds and the white men to their homes—

After, many saw Leatherlips rise on the anniversary of his murder on June 1. He then walked to the Scioto River and disappeared.

Haunted Buildings

Worley Building
Hoster Brewing Company
503 Front Street South
Columbus, Ohio 43215
39.951481,-83.001022

Smoky Shade of the Old Brew House

The Worley building served as the stable for the Hoster Brewing Company delivery wagon horses. During its brewing years, a woman was killed in a fire within and after, she appeared as a dark, smoky shade walking the hallways.

The Thurber House
77 Jefferson Avenue
Columbus, Ohio 43215
39.96592,-82.985182

Phantom Footsteps

James Thurber was an author and cartoonist who grew up in Columbus. For some time, his family lived on Jefferson Avenue, and the house was haunted. Thurber had a run-in with the ghost there. On November 17, 1915, when Thurber was 20-years-old, he had just finished bathing upstairs when he heard the sound of footsteps downstairs striding around the table in the dining room of his family home.

When he went to his brother's room to bring it to his attention, the steps increased, circling the table before they bounded up the stairway toward him. When he opened the door, there was nobody there.

It was no mystery what caused the sounds. The home sat on property once a part of the former Central Ohio Lunatic Asylum that burned down in the late 1860s. The fire killed six women. And in 1904, and before the family moved to the home, Thomas Tress, a Columbus jeweler, accidentally shot and killed himself in the house.

Now the Thurber House is a nonprofit literary arts center. The ghost continues to catch the attention of staff and visitors. A man in a collared shirt makes appearances occasionally, there are ghostly echoes of footsteps, and once in a while, someone receives a gentle poke.

The Westin Great Southern Columbus
310 S High Street
Columbus, Ohio 43215
39.955849, -82.999172

The Band Still Plays

The Great Southern Hotel & Theatre opened in the late 1800s, calling the building, *The Great Southern Fireproof Hotel and Opera House* as it was built from fireproof materials after fires destroyed five of the Columbus theaters. Sporadically, guests staying on the sixth floor call the front desk complaining about the boisterous band playing too loudly above them on the seventh floor where a ballroom once was and is no more.

**The Columbus Foundation
(Old Governor's Mansion)**
*1234 E Broad St
Columbus, Ohio 43205
39.966743, -82.96689*

Old Maid

The Old Governor's Mansion has seen many faces from its beginnings as the Lindenberg family home in 1904. It was home to ten Ohio governors beginning in 1919, and then, it would be a restaurant in the 1970s. Since 1988, it has housed The Columbus Foundation, a community improvement foundation. And yes, by the way, the occupants of this regal old building have shared their quarters with ghosts. From 1977 to 1981, the Mansion Restaurant made its home in the building.

During this time, a manager talking on the phone in her office saw an old black woman dressed in what appeared to be a blue maid's uniform pass by her doorway. When the manager arose to investigate, the woman had disappeared. After that, staff saw the same ghostly figure around the rooms and near the main stairway. But that is not all. The fusty scent of burning hair has filled the air, and pictures fall mysteriously from the walls.

Central Ohio Fire Museum
260 N. 4th Street
Columbus, Ohio 43215
39.968117, -82.996956

Whinnies in the Hall

Back in the early days of Columbus, volunteer firefighters consisted of twelve men, ages 15 to 50. They would divide into groups at a fire to do everything from guarding the property on fire to forming a bucket brigade, passing buckets from one to another until the last bucket holder could reach the fire.

As the city grew, so did the need for faster and more efficient equipment. To get volunteers, city authorities began paying the men in order of how quickly they showed up at the scene of the fire to help—five dollars to the first fireman to arrive, four dollars to the second man, and three dollars to the third. With the purchase of a steam fire engine in the mid-1800s and the need to house horses to pull it, the city hired a paid fire crew. Engine House Number 16 was an active City of Columbus firehouse from 1908 to 1981.

It was the last engine station built to house horses as the Columbus Fire Department began to transition to motorized equipment over the next ten years. It would be December of 1919 before the department's last horses were retired from this very building. Now, the structure is a fire museum and haunted, too, by the horses that once called it home. Those within have heard neighs, snorts, and whinnies echoing eerily through the halls. However, those who worry about the ghostly horses not receiving proper attention need not fret. The spirit of one of the first captains to work there, George Dukeman, haunts the museum. He was a meticulous man and made it painstakingly clear everything should be cared for, cleaned, and in its place. He was known to be particular about making sure someone tidied up the equipment in the upstairs. People have heard the sounds of the captain still working and singing to his chores. Lights go on and off, and shut doors bang open wide.

Columbus Public Health Department (Ohio State School for the Blind)

240 Parsons Avenue
Columbus, Ohio 43205
39.959174,-82.980628

Those Who Decided to Stay

The building between 1900 and 1920. Image: Library of Congress.

The sound of ghostly feet pound down the hallways of the three-story Columbus Public Health Department. Doors slam and specters peer around corners. It sounds terrifying, until you learn the noise comes from mischievous children who once filled the building and not murderous phantoms. From 1874 to 1953, the structure was the Ohio State School for the Blind, and those haunting it are the children who learned and stayed there. Those, that is, who decided to stay.

Ohio Statehouse
*1 Capitol Square
Columbus, Ohio 43215
39.961481,-82.999091*

Unfinished Dance

*Kate Chase, right, her father Salmon and sister.
Image: Library of Congress.*

Salmon Chase, a Cincinnati lawyer in the mid-1800s, was the elected governor of Ohio with aspirations of becoming president. Because Chase was without a wife, his doting daughter Kate became his official hostess at fifteen in Columbus while he was the governor and later in Washington after he was appointed treasury secretary.

She was well-qualified; after rivaling for her father's affections at age eight with his third wife, Kate was sent away to the country's most elite and exclusive private girls schools and taught all the graces of high society young women. At one event in 1859, legends are passed down that Abraham Lincoln, not yet president, and his wife, Mary, came to visit the Statehouse on a political campaign to begin working on common objectives with those who might be political rivals like Chase. During the evening festivities, which included a lavish Statehouse military ball, Kate (who was known to be quite flirtatious) advanced upon Abraham Lincoln and persuaded him to accompany her on the dance floor. A furious Mary Lincoln, who had met her husband at a cotillion herself in Springfield, Illinois, immediately stopped the band and escorted her husband from the floor. For the remainder of the two women's lives, they would each take turns refusing to attend certain events together. After death, Kate may have returned to cast a final blow—her ghost, along with the dead president Lincoln, has been seen promenading across the Statehouse floor, finally finishing their dance.

Jeffrey Mansion
165 Parkview Avenue
Columbus, Ohio 43209
39.972878,-82.944163

Ghostly Whistles

Unlike many of the spirits haunting Columbus, the Jeffrey Mansion has a mildly pleasant ghost attached to its property. The huge structure was built in 1905 as a family residence by industrialist Robert H. Jeffrey of the Jeffrey Manufacturing Company. The 34-acre estate boasted not only the English-style home, but also gardens and walkways. The mansion remained the home of the family from 1905 to 1941. In 1941, the estate donated the home and property to the City of Bexley on the condition that they are used for recreation and education. The city must be living up to the standards of the man who established his home. His ghost whistles contentedly around the building and grounds.

Schwartz Castle
492 S Third Avenue
Columbus, Ohio 43215
39.952451,-82.995701

The Undressed Ghost

Frederick Schwartz owned a reputable pharmacy in the 1800s. He built a large home, and when it was completed, he sent for his fiancé. Instead, she spurned the poor man.

Schwartz did not marry, became quite eccentric, and refused to cut his long hair. Sometimes local housewives complained that they had seen him sunbathing on the tower roof without clothing. After he died in 1914, passersby were startled by the nude ghost of a man appearing at the tower!

The Old Jury Room
22 E Mound Street
Columbus, Ohio 43215
39.955116,-82.99849

Dead Drunk

The Jury Room as it appeared in 1885 when the first stones for the old Franklin County Courthouse were laid. Courtesy: The Columbus Library

On the corner of Mound and Pearl, an old brick building stands that was the site of a gruesome killing. Twenty-six-year-old Paulus Rupprecht and two of his friends were drunk and returning from the theatre in March of 1859 when they passed a brothel owned by Frances Miller. When Miller refused his entrance, Rupprecht began kicking the door and banging it with his fists, demanding admission.

She ordered the disorderly man to leave, and he threatened the woman until she opened the door, drew a pistol, and shot him dead.

The Jury Room today.

For many years, the building was The Jury Room, a restaurant and bar. Staff and customers would see the shadow of a man moving around near the door, and hear muffled bangs before he vanished.

The Lofts Hotel
55 E Nationwide Boulevard
Columbus, Ohio 43215
39.968857,-83.00033

A Victorian Ghost

In the later 1800s, the Columbus Transfer Company built a storage warehouse at what is now The Lofts Hotel on East Nationwide Boulevard. It was later the Carr Plumbing and Supply Company, an architectural firm, and now a hotel. Mysteriously, it is not a plain-clothed worker showing up in spectral form and instead, guests and staff have reported a ghostly pale woman in a Victorian-era dress walking the first and second-floor hallways.

Cultural Arts Center
139 West Main Street
Columbus, Ohio 43215

Cultural Arts Center:
39.955425, -83.003334
*The gallows were located on what is now the
grassy knoll at the intersection of 2nd Street,
I-70 and W. Mound between the Juvenile
Detention Center and the electric station:*
39.954244,-83.002691

From the Gallows

Cultural Arts Center.

During the very early 1800s, there was a primitive penitentiary in Columbus. Just a couple blocks over on the corner of Mound and Scioto (Second) streets, there was the gallows. Although the prison moved within a few years and the city built an arsenal at the location, the gallows remained in the original area. Some believe that the old prison site is home to a haunting, and the reason is its nearness to the old execution grounds.

In the mid-1800s, 36-year-old William Young Graham was serving time at the Ohio Penitentiary for a highway robbery in June of 1841, before splitting the skull of guard Cyrus Sells while in prison for his earlier crime. Two years later, and during a prison fight, inmate 20-year-old Hester Foster beat a fellow prisoner to death with an iron shovel she had grabbed up from the fireplace to defend herself.

Location of the old gallows.

They were both sentenced to die and on February 9th, 1844, the sheriff, to save money, decided there would be a double hanging of the two. It was quite a sensation, with 10,000 curiosity-seekers, many of them drunk and unruly, traveling to the spot to watch the event. Officials hanged the pair, the crowds dispersed, and the city went back to normal.

Many years would pass. The city no longer carried out hangings in the streets, and the arsenal became the Cultural Arts Center. But something from the past worked its way from the ancient gallows and into the building, lingering there as if finding comfort in the old building.

Some who have worked there have seen a ghostly figure wearing the clothing of the 1840s during the time when little else was here on the outskirts of town. Although they are not sure, they have a pretty good idea that the ghost belongs to Hester Foster. I would bet that they keep a close eye on any tools lying around the facility and do not turn their backs on any shadows!

Fort Hayes
546 Jack Gibbs Boulevard
Columbus, Ohio 43215
39.972976,-82.987894

Lovelorn

There was once an armory, arsenal, and military training center in Columbus where Fort Hayes Metropolitan Education Center stands today. During the early years, a legend began of a young private who fell madly and deeply in love with his captain's daughter. The daughter loved the boy in return. However, the girl's father forbade the girl to see him. Still, the two continued to meet in secret, and the captain found out.

The young man's job was firing the cannon during the evening ceremonies in front of the barracks. During this time, John Wilkes Booth, a Confederate sympathizer, assassinated President Abraham Lincoln. Therefore, the cannon needed to be fired every minute during the day in honor of the fallen president. The captain knew this would overheat the gun, but he still called upon the young private to begin the commencements and had him do so late into the evening. Sometime during the firing, the cannon exploded with a fury killing the young private. Not long after, soldiers would see his lovelorn ghost walking the grounds where the cannon exploded as if searching for his sweetheart. Then he vanished.

**Greater Columbus
Antique Mall**
*1045 S. High Street
Columbus, Ohio 43206
39.940704, -82.997093*

Man With A Handlebar Mustache

The Greater Columbus Antique Mall was the residential home of a Bavarian soap and candle maker in the late 1800s, the Woodyard and J.I. Hughes Funeral Home in the 1920s, and later an Elks Lodge. Over the years, visitors to the building have heard mysterious noises in the upstairs, including footsteps. A man with a handlebar mustache, believed to be the original owner, walks the hallways. One shopper even watched as a spectral cat appeared and disappeared!

The Kelton House Museum and Garden
586 E Town Street
Columbus, Ohio 43215
39.961415,-82.984457

Smoker

There is an old mansion on Town Street built in 1852 by Fernando Cortez and Sophia Stone Kelton. It is now a museum and haunted. Georgeanne Reuter, Executive Director at Kelton House, relates that visitors see both male and female ghosts at the museum. As one staff worker stepped past the threshold of the front door, she remarked, "Well, I didn't know we had a historical reenactment at the museum today."

A second worker tipped her head and gave her a curious gaze and replied, "There isn't a reenactment." The first girl paled slightly and peered back out the door. "Oh." It seems she saw a Civil War soldier outside the building, leaning against the wall, and smoking a cigarette! He appeared as real to her as a flesh and blood person!

Ohio Theatre
39 East State Street
Columbus, Ohio 43215
39.960155,-82.999126

The Escape

Witnesses have seen an old lady looking down from the balcony in a longstanding building in Columbus. It is not just any building, though. It is the Ohio Theatre opened in 1928 and fantasy-themed, so those attending the vaudeville shows, stage shows, and movies could escape from the every day and into its glamorous grasp. Now, an early patron also takes a holiday from the afterlife there.

Mooney Mansion and
Calumet Bridge
259 Walhalla Road
Columbus Ohio 43202
40.025522, -83.007716

The Tall Tale

Teens once drove under the Calumet Street Bridge along Walhalla Street to look for the ghost of a man who died there. There was an abandoned mansion nearby belonging to a family named Mooney. Mister Mooney murdered his wife and daughter before killing himself by hanging on a beam of the bridge. Then he haunted the bridge, chasing those who drove past. If you paused near the bridge and a puddle had formed by the side of the road, you could see a reflection of the murdered wife and daughter when you looked within.

Although the Mooney family did live in the home for many years, and then it stood vacant for some time, there were no murders within the home. The urban legend that lured hundreds of teens to the area is believed to come from a real murder in the city, but not one at the mansion, which is private property.

Haunted River Areas

Scioto River Near
North Bank Park along Lower
Scioto Greenway
312 W Long Street
Columbus, Ohio 43215
39.964730, -83.015067

Bloody Island

Once near the location North Bank Park stands today, Bloody Island is gone, destroyed when the Army Corps of Engineers widened the Scioto River to aid in flood prevention. However, ghosts remain.

There once was a small island just before the meeting of the Olentangy River with the Scioto River in Columbus. On the shoreline close by, people have long told of hearing moans and cries. There is an explanation for the sounds—

The island went by many names—Brickell Island after the settler and landowner John Brickell, and then Willow Island for the trees that grew abundantly on its banks. But it would also gain a ghastly name later—*Bloody Island*.

During the late 1700s, the colonial governor of Virginia, Dunmore, declared war with the Indians as they attacked settlers along the Ohio River. He led a large army into Ohio, stopping in Circleville to camp. He then sent Colonel William Crawford and a few hundred riders to invade Indian villages along the Forks of Scioto, near Columbus' Arena District today.

As the militia came upon the village, it was clear that few men were around as they were on their first fall hunt. So the soldiers struck with a vengeance and easily so, outnumbering the old men, women, and children. With wild abandon, they rushed upon the unarmed villagers and began firing. The villagers, in a panic, started to flee in all directions. One woman was able to snatch up her five-year-old child and carry him to the safety of the willow-covered island nearby. She was quickly shot down and killed, but the child escaped into the trees and concealed himself in the hollow of a sycamore.

When the warriors returned two days later, they discovered the little one still safely tucked into its grasp. Yet, most of their family members were murdered and left dead on the shores covered in blood. Many years would pass where nobody lived near the banks. Then as the land was settled, and later the city grew, the gruesome cries of those villagers who died there began to echo eerily in the wind.

You can access the Lower Scioto Greenway at North Bank Park and walk near the area of the long-gone island, although it may be difficult to see the waterway seasonally.

North Bank Park hike along Lower Scioto Greenway

311 W Long Street

Columbus, Ohio 43215

39.965347, -83.010015 to

39.965635, -83.015288

Along the Olentangy River
Columbus, Ohio 43215

British Island

Up the Olentangy River, there was once a small island. During the War of 1812, British soldiers defeated at the Thames River in Canada were kept prisoner here. Muddy and flooded, it was a miserable place for the men. Sometime during their stay, some soldiers decided to escape and began to swim across the river. They were almost to the banks when their captors shot them dead. For years after, witnesses heard splashing, yells, and groans creeping from the water where the men were murdered.

Haunted Parks

Schiller Park
1000 City Park Avenue
Columbus, Ohio 43206
39.942094, -82.993558

Headless Ghost in City Park

The area around Schiller Statue where a man was killed—and returned.

In November of 1894, a 54-year-old wine agent for Brandt and Company in Toledo named Albert Dittelbach was visiting the city of Columbus for business. Those around him noticed he was rather downcast, but no one expected to find him dead in the popular Schiller Park in German Village in front of Schiller's statue. He had shot himself in the head.

On Friday, November 30 and less than two weeks after Dittelbach's death, two young men—William Bell and a friend—were returning from a party and took a shortcut through the dark, deserted park. Just within the bounds of the park, they noticed a figure draped in a gray robe from shoulders to knees. He was pacing back and forth along the walkway directly in front of the Schiller Monument. Strangely, his hands were outstretched and flailing about as if blindly trying to reach for something. Curious, the two paused to take in the lone stranger as he came closer and closer. To their horror, they saw he had no head.

Glen Echo Park
510 Cliffside Drive
Columbus, Ohio 43202
40.018815, -82.999410

The Ladened Rope

Glen Echo Park and Glen Echo Creek.

In February of 1916, a 75-year-old farmer named John Smith cut a hole in the ice of the stream at Glen Echo Park. He tied one end of a rope to a tree root, and he fastened the free end around his ankles. He then dove into the water headfirst.

The next morning, two boys came upon the rope bound to the tree root and followed it to a section of ice on the water that was not as frozen as the rest. With great effort, the curious boys tugged on the ladened rope, pulling until the man's body came to the surface feet first. Since that time, passersby have seen the old farmer's ghost pacing back and forth along the creek's edge. He then leans over and fiddles with something at his feet before rising and diving into a deeper section of water headfirst, disappearing.

Old State Penitentiary Grounds
McFerson Park
*175 Nationwide Boulevard
Columbus, Ohio 43215
39.968278, -83.007495*

Ohio Penitentiary

The old Ohio State Penitentiary.

Many years ago, a prison stretched from nearly the Scioto River from West Street to Neil and across Nationwide Arena. Passersby occasionally catch the scent of fire and hear screams where it once stood. Others witness shadowy figures stumbling along the sidewalks. Most are shocked when someone tells them the cause for these mysterious sights, smells, and sounds.

The prison was operated from 1834 to 1984. During this time and in April of 1930, a fire broke out on the roof after inmates were locked into their cells for the night. Almost 322 prisoners were trapped inside, most of them living four to a cell, and died from burns and inhaling the poisonous gases. Although much of the blame was made through the media that the fire was started by inmates planning an escape, the actual cause may never be known. Defective electric wiring, a gas torch accidentally left on, and spontaneous ignition of the wood were also cited as possible causes of the fire, deaths, and thereafter, ghosts.

The Ohio State Penitentiary in 1990. Image: Library of Columbus.

At rear is the arch from the Union Depot (moved to this area) leading into McFerson Park and the area of The Death House— housing the electric chair and inmates sentenced to death.

Topiary Garden in Deaf School Park
480 East Town Street
Columbus, Ohio 43215
39.961366, -82.987568

Shadow

Until the Deaf School began in 1829 on Broad and High Streets, children who were deaf or hard of hearing had few choices regarding schooling except to pay high tuition and move far from family and out of state. With the gentle goading of a compassionate minister, Reverend James Hoge, the wheels began churning for a centrally located deaf school in Ohio.

Ohio institution for the education of the deaf. Image: The New York Public Library.

Officials purchased ten acres for a site in 1829 on East Town Street in Columbus, and the first building opened in 1834. By 1941, the buildings were in grave disrepair, and the school moved to a new site. However, ghostly remnants of its past remain. A landscaped park with picnic tables and a walkway with a topiary garden have taken over the area where the school and property stood. Visitors to the park see shadow figures walking around the old grounds and the sidewalks surrounding the park.

Haunted Bars & Restaurants

Elevator Brewery and Draught Haus
161 North High Street
Columbus, Ohio 43215
39.965642,-83.001477

Footprints in the Snow

The Bott Bros Billiards. Image: Columbus Public Library

On the corner of North High and West Lafayette streets, a few blocks from Nationwide Arena, there is a building that once housed Bott Brother's Billiards and a gentleman's saloon in the early 1900s. Just outside was a clock to mark the time for those who passed by. The pub was a very popular place for men to socialize and entertain themselves and contained a billiards room, pub, and a restaurant.

During this time, a horrible murder happened there in the winter and during a heavy snowfall. A man who had been visiting the pub stepped outside to make his way home at 10:05 p.m. As he pushed the door open, someone slipped from the shadows and thrust a knife deep into his chest. When the men inside realized what had occurred, they raced outside to find the fleeing attacker. Strangely, though, the only tracks they could see that led to the doorway where the killer had stopped were the small imprints of a woman's bare feet.

The man died, authorities never found the murderer, and the clock outside the pub stuck at the time of the man's death at 10:05 p.m. until city workers later replaced it. Now the pub is the well-known Elevator Brewery and Draught Haus. The man's ghost wanders within the building. And occasionally, during a dusting of snow, tiny bare footprints appear mysteriously in front of the doors.

Barley's Brewing Company
467 N High Street
Columbus, Ohio 43215
39.97199,-83.002828

Unrested

There is also a brewpub on High Street sitting on top of the Old North Cemetery. Occasionally at night, the unrested ghosts beneath their floors move things around inside the doors.

Char Bar
439 N. High Street
Columbus, Ohio 43215
39.971373,-83.002869

Dark Form

After some of the dead were reburied in other cemeteries, the land where the Old North Graveyard stood began to become industrialized. In 1873, Columbus had far outgrown its first Union Train Station on the east side of North High Street. By 1875, the railroad built a larger brick station farther north along High Street to replace the old wooden building, including waiting rooms and ticket offices. In addition, 42 passenger trains would depart from the depot per day along 13 different train tracks.

A dark tunnel beneath High Street was once used to divert foot and carriage traffic away from the dangerous train tracks. Collection of DAK—1888.

There was always congestion of foot traffic and wagons stopping to wait for trains to pass. Carriages working their way along High Street were backed up for nearly seven hours to get from one side of the busy railway tracks to the other. To reduce traffic in 1875, the city built a tunnel underpass beneath the mass of tracks so streetcars and horse carts could pass unhindered by the continuous line of trains. It was a two-lane passageway 550 feet long. The tunnel featured drainage, sidewalks on both sides, and was lighted by gas lamps.

It was only a few months into its heyday when both pedestrians and horse-drawn carriage drivers snubbed its use. It was far easier for those on foot to worry about the dangers of crossing paths with the trains above than the labor of ascending and descending the steps through the tunnels to get to the other side. Even though a sturdy mule was waiting to help any horses make their way up the steep incline, it was still difficult for carriage horses with their loads to make their way up and down the passageway.

It was only made worse with the lack of ventilation and the stench of manure left behind by the many animal-led carriages passing through.

This very tunnel and the previous graveyard were right along the same section of the street where the Char Bar building was erected around 1900. The tunnel was replaced with an overpass. Trains were diverted beneath. The ground floors of many buildings along High Street that were once level with the roadway were now underground.

A door and a window that once opened up to the street level before the viaduct was built is now only open to the darkness beyond. There is a ladder on the other side leading to the dark tunnel. And a lone, ghostly figure lurks here.

Some visiting the rustic brick pub have seen a dark form in the cellar area where the restrooms and old tunnel are found that is believed to be an unrested spirit from the cemetery or a ghostly pedestrian returning after being hit and killed by a long-gone train.

The haunted piano at Char Bar.

Employees say that girls go down to the restrooms five or six at a time to hear an old piano down there that plays on its own.

Ringside Café
19 N Pearl Street
Columbus, Ohio 43215
39.963167,-82.999941

Clem Haunts the Building

What started as the Board of Trade Saloon in 1897 became the Chamber of Commerce Cafe and Rathskeller after it burned down in 1909. It was also the Jolly Gargoyle during the speakeasy years. The bar was finally christened Clem's Ringside Cafe in 1960 by Clem Amorose, a former owner. Clem haunts the building. Patrons see his shadowy shape seated in his favorite booth.

Schmidt's Sausage Haus And Restaurant
240 E Kossuth Street
Columbus, Ohio 43206
39.946398,-82.991195

The Overseer

J. Fred Schmidt opened his business in German Village in 1886 as a meatpacking house. In 1914, the family opened a concession stand at the Ohio State Fair. Later, his grandson, George F. Schmidt, opened Schmidt's first restaurant around the corner from his family's meatpacking house. J. Fred Schmidt is still around in ghostly form, overseeing the establishment. He is seen as an elderly man waving amicably in a mirror and 'felt' by workers who get a certain sensation someone or something is watching them.

Haunted Railways and Roadways

***Near Greater Columbus
Convention Center
(Old Union Depot)***
*370 N High Street
Columbus, Ohio 43215
39.970540, -83.002265*

Lincoln Ghost Train

The Old Nashville.
The Engine that drew Lincoln's Funeral Train from Washington to Springfield, Ill.

In April 1865, the train carrying the coffin of President Lincoln traveled from Washington, D.C., to Springfield, Illinois, for the president's burial. It arrived in Columbus on Saturday, April 29th, 1865, around 7:30 a.m. at the Union Depot (location of convention center) and departed at 8:00 p.m. Between, workers removed the coffin from the train car and placed it on a hearse drawn by six white horses that took the corpse to the Statehouse for viewing.

Thousands watched as the train passed, and years later, it made more spirited processions along the old route. Occasionally, in April the ghostly train returns to Columbus. It is draped in long lengths of black cloth, and spectral faces peer out the window at those who watch it pass.

Watkins Road Bridge
2820 Watkins Road
Columbus, Ohio 43207
39.903797,-82.916724

Headless Hattie Bridge

Near Sycamore Creek Park, Watkins Road crosses Alum Creek. Years ago and during the logging boom, the Spangler sawmill sat here. It had a ripsaw and circular saw for processing logs to lumber and a grinding stone for area farmers to grind their grain. It was a popular place, and plenty of carriages came across Alum Creek at this point. It is still busy. Now instead of horses and wagons working over a wooden bridge, motorcycles and cars cross over a concrete viaduct.

Occasionally at dusk, a vehicle slows, much to the irritation of those driving behind, so the driver can honk the horn and wait for Headless Hattie to appear. Hattie was a woman who was decapitated here during an accident many years ago and whose head hovers above the hood of cars passing and honking three times.

Haunted Colleges

Ohio State University Pomerene Hall and Mirror Lake
Columbus, Ohio 43210
39.998047, -83.014343

Lady of the Lake

Pomerene Hall has the ghost of Professor Frederick Clark. Despondent over lost mine investments, the 45-year-old man shot himself in a field near the north dormitory on a September morning of 1903. A farmhand found the body at the root of a tree. After, Clark's ghost rambled around Pomerene Hall, making loud noises, slamming doors, and following students with the sound of his footsteps clacking behind them.

His wife suffered greatly over the death of her husband. She blamed the university for not doing more to help him and swore she would return to haunt the university after her death many years later. After she died, students began to see a woman wearing a dress floating across Mirror Lake, near Pomerene Hall, with a mist around her.

Ohio State University
Orton Hall
155 South Oval Mall
Columbus, Ohio 43210
39.998402,-83.011903

Lonely Lantern Light

Orton Hall was named after Ohio State's first president and a professor of Geology from 1873-1899, Doctor Edward Orton. Orton enjoyed reading by lantern light in the tower. Even though he is long-dead, students have seen the lights from his ghostly lantern flickering through the slots.

Ohio State University
Orton Hall
155 South Oval Mall
Columbus, Ohio 43210
39.998402,-83.011903

Gargoyles

Sometimes, passersby report the heads of the gargoyles on Orton Hall moving.

Columbus State Community College Grounds
550 E Spring Street
Columbus, Ohio 43215
39.968372,-82.986517

College Above the City of the Dead

There have been complaints of strange noises and lights flickering at the college campus. Most of the events happen at night and both security officers and patrolmen in the area have been startled by disturbances they cannot explain. *It can be explained.* There was once a Catholic cemetery on the grounds of the college with approximately 4000 burials between 1846 and 1874. Eventually, a new cemetery was developed farther outside the city, and those with family buried here were asked to move their dead kin. Some did. But not all were moved before, in 1905, St. Patrick's College was plopped on the hallowed ground. And later, Columbus State Community College.

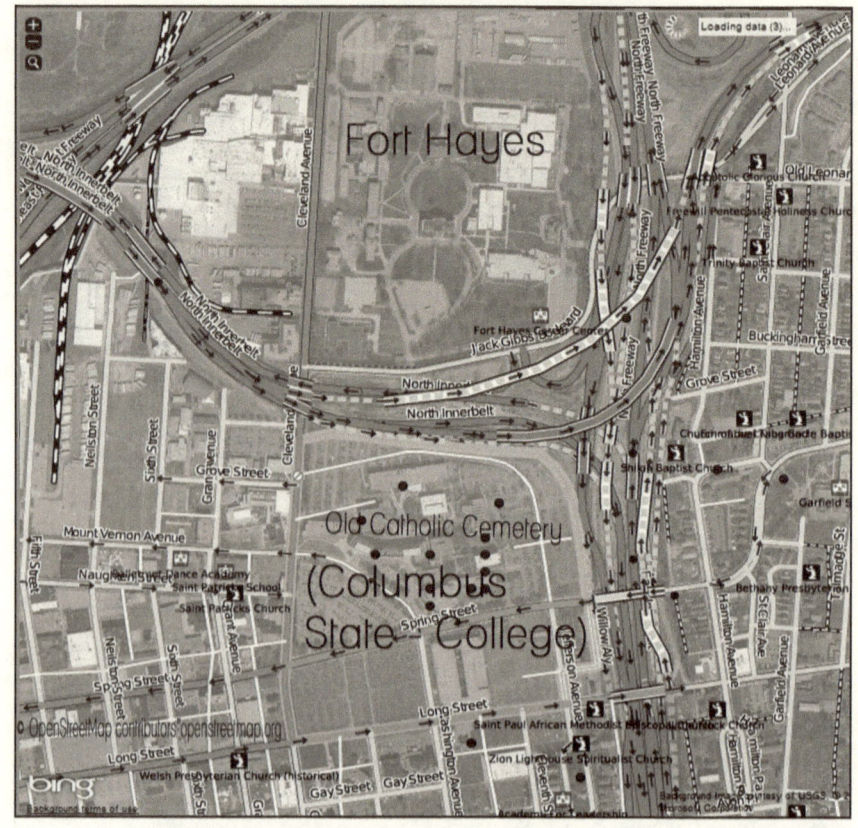

**Area of Old Catholic Cemetery—1848-1888
(Some bodies moved to Green Lawn)**

Not Far from Columbus...

Little Pennsylvania Cemetery
7700 London-Groveport Road
Grove City, Ohio 43123
39.850457,-83.201194

The Woolly-Booger

Little Pennsylvania Cemetery has also been called Woolyburger Cemetery, Woolybooger Cemetery, and Willie Butcher's Cemetery.

Big Darby Creek runs 84 miles, and along its route, it passes through the town of Darbydale. Just outside Darbydale is an ancient cemetery, Little Pennsylvania Cemetery, where people like the Atheys, Hambletons, and Bouchers have found their final resting place. As small as it is with a little over 200 graves, the cemetery still has many stories conjured up about it for over half a century.

Some spoke of a Bigfoot seen in the area—as they call them in the south, a Woolly Booger or hairy man. Others whispered that a man butchered his family and killed himself, only to return from the grave as a boogeyman. Some called this revenant Wooly Booger, and he wreaked out vengeance on anyone entering his family plot. Then fingers pointed to a certain headstone belonging to Willie Boucher because, well, it sounded kind of like Woolly Booger. Certainly, he was the killer. Yet, Willie was only a one year old when he died.

Willie's Grave.

Still, there might have been a boogeyman there. In the spring of 1957, the half-clothed corpse of a young woman was found on a lover's lane road by Big Darby Creek near Darbydale by four teens heading out to fly fish. The murderer had wrapped a towel around the body before stuffing it in a feed sack and dumping it into a puddle of water. Police had a tough time finding out who murdered the girl, and many-a-parent probably warned their children from Columbus, past Darbydale, and beyond that they better be in by dark because there was a boogeyman on the loose near Darbydale. And they were right.

**Studio 35 Cinema
and Drafthouse**
*3055 Indianola Avenue
Clintonville, Ohio 43202
40.026053,-83.001818*

Dying to see a Movie

Movie-goers have seen a man dressed in a military uniform from the 1930s seated amongst them that is certainly not of the living. Most say the man must be from the Depression era and some even believe he died inside the building while watching a movie.

Little Theatre Off Broadway
3981 Broadway
Grove City, Ohio 43123
39.883314,-83.093208

Ethel

Ethel King was nearly blind when she played the piano for silent movies at King Theatre in Grove City. Ethel's mother accompanied her, instructing the young woman when to emphasize certain points of the show, slowing down and speeding up according to the action and plot transformation. King Theatre later became Little Theatre Off Broadway. It has a ghost and many believe it is Ethel. Doors slam, and footsteps echo in the rooms. Volunteers have even seen an apparition believed to be the piano player.

Longfellow Elementary
120 Hiawatha Avenue
Westerville, Ohio 43081
40.118072,-82.933216

She Walks The Halls

Longfellow Elementary has the ghost of a woman who walks the hallways to the beat of her clacking heels.

Pioneer Cemetery
865 S State Street
Westerville, Ohio 43081
40.105255,-82.925041

Pioneer Ghosts

Now surrounded by modern businesses, the old Pioneer Cemetery, established in 1817, is home to a few souls still wandering around. Look closely at these pictures to see ghostly figures just outside the cemetery fence.

Henry Street
S Henry Street
Delaware, Ohio 43015
40.295976, -83.064468

The Red Slipper Murder

Henry Street in Delaware where a ghostly murder victim walks.

A squirrel hunter found the mysterious girl's body clad only in a flannel nightgown and red, one-strap slippers on September 18th, 1953. She was dumped near a deserted roadside along Route 53 in Wyandot County 3 miles north of Upper Sandusky, her face so severely crushed that it was unidentifiable. Local police traced the serial number inside the red slippers from Columbus shoe manufacturer Prima Footwear that distributed their products to a department store in White Plains, New York. Unofficial police reports from White plains showed a young woman, blue-eyed Cynthia Pfeil, had been missing since August 24th. With a photo of Cynthia in hand, police marched to the department store where the slippers had been purchased.

One clerk recalled selling the shoes to the girl only two days before she disappeared. Shortly after, the police headed to the home of Cynthia's parents, who stated they were unsure of their daughter's whereabouts. However, they believed she was with a boyfriend, Roger Schinagle, whom they did not approve of, but Cynthia had met when they attended the university together a year ago. Police brought in slim, clean-cut, and sandy-haired Roger Schinagle, age 19 and a Ohio Wesleyan sophomore, for questioning shortly after; he hardly fit the profile of a murderer. But they did not know his dark and jealous side. Cynthia had returned home after her freshman year and began work in Cleveland. Roger worked for a trucking company, and when he was not in school, he drove through Cleveland to see her.

Cynthia snuck down to see Roger in Delaware, divulging she had to tell him something. He set her up in the equipment shed at the south athletic field on the campus because she could not afford a hotel room. Roger would not allow her to leave as he did not want anyone to know she was there and demanded she not leave the shed. But Cynthia did not heed his words, grew restless at being cooped up, and wandered out to the field. A groundskeeper spotted the girl and hastily informed Roger that he knew she was staying there. Angry, Roger returned, dragged Cynthia back inside the small building, and beat her so furiously with a lead pipe, he killed her. He then dumped her body in an isolated area 35 miles away from campus.

Roger Schinagle went to prison for ten years and was released. Her family buried 19-year-old Cynthia in White Plains. She had been two months pregnant at the time of the murder, and Roger admitted the child was his own. But her story is far from over. Cynthia walks Henry Street near her murder site in a flannel nightgown and red, one-strap slippers. Some have even heard her wailing as she strolls along the route.

Perkins Observatory
3199 Columbus Pike
Delaware, Ohio 43015
40.251134,-83.055739

The Watcher

Occasionally, those visiting Perkins Observatory see a tall, lanky figure walking around the building and grounds on clear, starry nights. Then the form suddenly vanishes. Nowadays, few know to whom the ghostly form belongs; he died nearly a hundred years ago. But in the late 1800s, he was a solid figure in the community. His name was Hiram Perkins.

Hiram Perkins grew up on a pig farm in Madison County, then went to Ohio Wesleyan University, where he graduated with a degree in Math and Astronomy. He taught for a while at the college, then as the school's budget began getting cramped during the Civil War, he left his job so another faculty member could have his position.

He returned home to help his family raise hogs to sell to the Union Army, and being frugal, made a fortune from this venture. After the war, Hiram returned to his teaching at the university and later on bequeathed a lifetime of savings and investments to build Perkins Student Observatory. He died at the age of 90 before the building was completed. But he returns now to oversee the grounds along with the observatory.

Citations

Berliner Park:
Travel Tips © USA TODAY, a division of Gannett Co. Inc. http://
traveltips.usatoday.com/bike-paths-columbus-ohio-102894.html
Camp Chase:
The National magazine: an illustrated monthly, Volume 46, Let's Talk
This Over—Info on Ransburg
The Washington Post, June 16, 1917 Veiled Lady of Camp Chase,"
Dramatic Figure of Reunion, Wildly Cheered by Dixie's Sons
Library of Congress: LC-DIG-ppmsca-15835
Char Bar:
2013 ColumbusRailroads.com. http://columbusrailroads.com. The
Columbus Horsecar System - 1863-1892, and The
Street Railway Companies of Columbus, Ohio 1863-1892 Steiner, Rowlee.
"A Review of Columbus Railroads", 1952, unpublished 125 page
manuscript available from the library of the Ohio Historical Society, 1982
Velma Drive, Columbus, Ohio 43211
Fire Museum:
Special thanks to Bill Hall Retired Firefighter and fire department
historian for Columbus, Columbus Fire Department History 1822 to
2012.
Library of Congress Prints and Photographs LOT 10869
Evening Gazette - Wednesday, May 07, 1919, Xenia, Ohio - Columbus Fire
Mounts to Nine
Elyria Chronicle - May 6, 1919 - A Disastrous Fire Sweeps Columbus -
Columbus , May 6
Columbus Health Department:
Columbus Public Health Department - Ohio School for the Blind
Columbus Public Health, 240 Parsons Avenue Columbus, Ohio
publichealth.columbus.gov/columbus-public-health-history.aspx
Dictionary of Ohio Historic Places Somerset Publishers Inc,
Ohio Exploration Society William Martin, History of Franklin County: A
Collection of Reminiscences of the Early
Settlement of the County (Columbus, 1858).
Cultural Arts Center, Ohio Pen and Statehouse:
Statehood to Statehouse - Ohio Legislative Service Commission
HISTORY OF THE City of Columbus Capital of Ohio, BY ALFRED B: lee, A.
M.
From the Outlook Weekly, October 26, 2006 HAUNTED COLUMBUS,
October 26, 2006 - By Rob Maxon
History of Franklin County: A Collection of Reminiscences of the Early
Settlement of the County : with Biographical Sketches and a Complete
History of the County to the Present Time - William T. Martin,
Published:January 1858 Publisher:Follett, Forster & Co
Lorain Republican - Wednesday, February 14, 1844, Elyria, Ohio
The Stark County Democrat., December 12, 1905, WEEKLY EDITION,
(Canton, Ohio) 1833-1912
Forgotten Ohio, http://www.forgottenoh.com/Counties/Franklin/
culturalarts.html
Ohio Statehouse:
Amarillo Globe-Times - Monday, October 03, 1960, Amarillo, TX
A Story of Kate Chase's Family - By Paul LeRoy Hacker p 14
http://www.thisweeknews.com/content/stories/germanvillage/
news/2009/09/30/1001geghost_ln.html
Deaf School:
Ohio School for the Deaf - ohioschoolforthedeaf.org/history.aspx
Glenn Echo Park:
Columbus Evening Dispatch - Sunday, June 27, 1909, Columbus, Ohio
Evening Independent - Monday, August 19, 1957, Massillon, Ohio
Findlay Republican Courier - Friday, June 12, 1964, Findlay, Ohio
Piqua Leader-Dispatch - Friday, September 22, 1911, Piqua, Ohio

Franklinton Cemetery:
Insiders' Guide to Columbus, Ohio, 2nd By Shawnie Kelley
Old North Cemetery:
Chronicle Telegram - Monday, May 21, 2001, Elyria, Ohio
http://www.genealogybug.net/Franklin_Cemeteries/misc/north.htm -
Leona L. Gustafson - North Graveyard (aka Old North) Columbus,
Franklin County, Ohio
Ohio Penitentiary:
HEALTH ISSUES AND MEDICAL CARE IN THE OHIO PENITENTIARY:
1833-1907
Nancy E. Tatarek*, Amy L. Harris, and Dorothy E. Dean Ohio University -
Department of Sociology & Anthropology drc.ohio.gov/web/histop.htm -
Inside the Pen - By David Lore The Columbus Dispatch October 28, 1984
The Enquirer Sources: Ohio Department of Rehabilitation and Correction,
Death Penalty Information Center Inside the Pen - By David Lore The
Columbus Dispatch October 28, 1984 Reprinted with permission from
The Columbus (Ohio) Dispatch http://in-and-around-columbus.com/
arena-district-arch.html November 20, 2008 - Arch Not from Ohio Pen
yet Union Station
Casstevens, Frances H. "Ohio State Penitentiary." Out of the Mouth of Hell.
Jefferson:
McFarland and Company, 2005. 137-52.
Report on the Ohio State Penitentiary Fire April 21, 1930 - Ohio
Inspection Bureau. T.B.
Sellers, Manager,Columbus Ohio
Ohio Historical Society, . "Ohio Penitentiary Fire-Ohio History Central-A
product of the Ohio Historical Society." (2010): n. pag. Web. 12 Apr 2010.
www.ohiohistorycentral.org/image.php?rec=558&img=969
http://www.prairieghosts.com/oh-osp.html
The Commonplace Book -Notes and images from the Old Northwest of
past and present.
The Death of Colonel William Crawford: 230 Years Ago by Dan Wilkens
History of Franklin County: A Collection of Reminiscences of the Early
Settlement of the County : with Biographical Sketches and a Complete
History of the County to the Present Time - William T. Martin, Published
Clayton Murder: Coshocton Daily Times 1908
Ohio Theatre:
CAPA 55 East State Street, Columbus, Ohio 43215-4264- www.capa.com/
ohio-theatre/theatre-history
Central Ohio Hauntings - 2006 Nellie Kampmann www.eeriecanal.org/
centralohiohaunts.html
Bloody Island and British Island:
The fight that forged Ohio - Often overlooked, War of 1812 secured state's
future - he Dispatch Printing Company
http://theshadowlands.net/places/ohio.htm
Elevator Brewery:
Fort Hayes:
Greater Columbus Antique Mall:
http://www.ohioexploration.com/inv06opn70212.htm
http://www.centralohioparanormalresearchgroup.com/
GreaterColumbusantiquemall.html
www.columbusunderground.com/explore-columbus-greater-columbus-
antique-mall
Staff and workers, Greater Columbus Antique Mall
Centennial history of Columbus and Franklin County, Ohio, Volume 2 By
Green Lawn Abbey:
www.thehenryford.org/exhibits/pic/1996/oct.html -The Henry Ford
Green Lawn Cemetery:
Drug Stimulated Affair Ends With Both Lovers Dead - Odessa American,
February 27, 1958, Odessa Texas

Cross Examine Dr. J. H. Snook - Biloxi Daily Herald Friday August 9, 1929, Biloxi Mississippi Snook Paid For His Life for An Outstanding Brutal Crime - Times Recorder, Saturday March 01, 1930, Zanesville, Ohio
Greenlawn Cemetery- The ghost of Dr. James H. Snook,
www.forgottenoh.com/Greenlawn/snook.html
GOLD MEDAL KILLER The Shocking True Story of the Ohio State Professor – an Olympic Champion – and His Coed Lover - DIANA BRITT FRANKLIN WITH NANCY PENNELL
Short North Gazette - The Trial of Dr. James Howard Snook Sept 1999 by Nancy Patzer
Leatherlips:
The Hesperian of the West; A Monthly Miscellany of General Literature Otway Curry, Columbus, Ohio, 1838. Edited by William Davis Gallagher. Volume 3 (The accusers were those known as Tecumseh and his brother, the Prophet.) His death occurred on June 1 or 2, 1810.
Historic Cemeteries:
South and East:
http://www.genealogybug.net/Franklin_Cemeteries/city_graveyards/page037.htm and The Columbus City Graveyards Content © 1985 by Donald M. Schlegel
Camp Chase Articles Southeast Cemetery Transfer to Camp Chase - Information compiled by Dennis Ranney
www.genealogybug.net/Franklin_Cemeteries/city_graveyards/page007.htm
Lincoln Funeral Train:
The Lincoln Highway National Museum & Archives 102 Old Lincoln Way West Galion, Ohio 44833
Above Top Secret: Ghostly Lincoln Funeral Train abovetopsecret.com/
Hamilton Township High School:
Andrew Henderson, ForgottenOH.com
Jeffrey Mansion:
Rubio, Josie. "Ghost Stories." Columbus Dispatch: Columbus Monthly Oct. 2003
Longfellow Elementary School:
Ohio Exploration Society—Franklin County
Ohio History Central-http://www.ohiohistorycentral.org/entry.php?rec=820
The Highland weekly news., August 26, 1875, page 2
Schwartz Castle:
A Historical Guidebook to Old Columbus: Finding the Past in the Present in Ohio's Capital City by Bob Hunter, Lucy S. Wolfe, Ohio University Press; 1 edition (October 18, 2012)
Jury Room:
Deed of Land held by Steven K. Imm. Columbus Dispatch 5/6/1979 p.E-1
Columbus Register of Historic Properties OH720.288/C726, p. CR-47
BooRah, An Intuit companyhttp://business.intuit.com
Historic Preservation Officer- City of Columbus Planning Division
Historic Columbus Taverns: The Capital City's Most Storied Saloons Tom Betti Doreen Uhas Sauer
Fremont journal (Fremont, OH) 1859-04-08 [p]. - seq-3.p
The Daily press. (Cincinnati [Ohio], April 02, 1859, Image 2
Little Theatre Off Broadway:
Cinema Treasures—http://cinematreasures.org/theaters/25526
Grove City Record-This Week Community News—Ghostly sightings at theater By SARAH SOLE
Grove City (Images of America: Ohio) by Janet Shailer, Laura Lanese
The Lofts:
The Lofts, 55 East Nationwide Blvd.—http://www.55lofts.com/history.asp
Farm Implement News, Volume 13, page 16
http://www.ohioexploration.com/franklincounty.htm

Mooney Mansion and Walhalla Lane:
Franklin County Auditors Office records
Ancestry.com—1940s census
www.sleepyhollowpumpkins.com/legend_mooneymansion.htm
Beck's School and Franklin County Infirmary: Centennial History of
Columbus and Franklin County, Ohio, Volume 1 By William Alexander
A Haunted History of Columbus, Ohio — By Nellie Kampmann
History of Franklin County: POOR HOUSE, OR INFIRMARY- http://
www.genealogybug.net/franklin_1858/infirmary.htm:Leona L.
Gustafson
INVENTORY OF THE COUNTY ARCHIVES OF OHIO NO. 40. FRANKLIN
COUNTY (COLUMBUS) Prepared by The Ohio Historical Records Survey
Project Service Division Work Projects Administration Columbus, Ohio
The Ohio Historical Records Survey Project 1942
Ringside Café:
Columbus Library.org– Central Ohio Buildings
Schmidt's Sausage Haus/Restaurant:
Columbus 1910-1970 by Richard E. Barrett OH977.13 C72 B274col p.97
Columbus
Westin:
Photos: Haunted places around Columbus. (n.d.). The Columbus
Dispatch. https://www.dispatch.com/photogallery/oh/20191023/
photogallery/102309996/PH/1
Thurber House:
The Evening Telegraph (Philadelphia, Pa.)1868-11-19 [p8]
My Life and Hard Times-James Thurber
Forgotten Ohio forgottenoh.com/Counties/Franklin/thurber.html
Ballou's Pictorial Drawing-Room Companion, page 376, View of the
Lunatic Asylum, Columbus Ohio - Ballou, Maturin Murray, 1820-1895.
"View of the Lunatic Asylum, Columbus, Ohio", a wood engraving
published November 1857 in "Ballou's Pictorial Drawing-Room
companion", Boston, Massachusetts. Designed by Nathan Kelley, it
opened in 1838.
http://www.thurberhouse.org/his-life-and-times.html
Franklin County Court House:
"A Brief History of Franklin County's Courthouses" By Robert C. Van
Schoyck Upper Arlington News, October 1st, 2003 page 36A
 Cemetery Map Directions with aid of: http://www.genealogybug.net/
Franklin_Cemeteries/city_graveyards/page037.htm and The Columbus
City Graveyards Content © 1985 by Donald M. Schlegel

www.ingramcontent.com/pod-product-compliance
Lightning Source LLC
Chambersburg PA
CBHW051308250626
47155CB00009B/3480